Echo and the Bat Pack

THE THING IN THE SEWERS

text by Roberto Pavanello
translated by Marco Zeni

STONE ARCH BOOKS
a capstone imprint

First published in the United States in 2012
by Stone Arch Books
A Capstone Imprint
1710 Roe Crest Drive
North Mankato, Minnesota 56003
www.capstonepub.com

Text by Roberto Pavanello
Original cover and illustrations by Blasco Pisapia and Pamela Brughera
Graphic Project by Laura Zuccotti and Gioia Giunchi

© 2007 Edizioni Piemme S.p.A., via Tiziano 32 - 20145 Milano- Italy
International Rights © Atlantyca S.p.A., via Leopardi, 8 — 20123 Milano, Italy —
foreignrights@atlantyca.it

Original Title: IL MOSTRO DELLE FOGNE

Translation by: Marco Zeni

www.batpat.it

Library of Congress Cataloging-in-Publication Data is available on the Library of
Congress website.

ISBN: 978-1-4342-4247-1 (hardcover)
ISBN: 978-1-4342-3824-5 (library binding)

Summary: Echo and the Bat Pack must solve the mystery of the thing living in
Fogville's sewers.

Designer: Emily Harris

Printed in China
0412/CA21200581
042012   006679

TABLE OF CONTENTS

HELLO THERE!

I'm your friend Echo, back again to tell you about one of the Bat Pack's adventures!

Do you know what I do for a living? I'm a writer, and scary stories are my specialty. Creepy stories about witches, ghosts, and graveyards. But I'll tell you a secret — I am a real scaredy-bat!

First of all, let me introduce you to the Bat Pack. These are my friends. . . .

Becca

Age: 10

Loves all animals (including bats, toads, and anything else gross)

An excellent actress

Michael

Age: 12

Smart, thoughtful, and good at solving problems

Doesn't take no for an answer

Tyler

Age: 11

Computer genius

Funny and adventurous, but scared of his own shadow

Dear fans of scary stories,

Imagine that you are out on a walk one day and you run into two very different animals. One is an enormous fire-breathing dragon, and the other is a teeny, tiny white kitten. Which do you think you'd be more likely to reach out and pet?

The kitten? Wrong answer! In reality, that dragon acts more like a puppy who loves to be petted. It will throw itself at your feet, wagging its tail and begging to play. (Watch out for that tail, by the way — it's 16 feet long!) The kitten, on the other hand, is an adult male of the *Evilus Clawus* family, a species that could tear you to pieces with just a few swipes of its paw!

Think I'm making this all up? Of course I am! I'm a writer, after all!

Truthfully, I gave you this example because the story I'm about to tell made me think of something my mother always said. "Fur-ball," she would say (that was her nickname for me), "always remember, 'When bats are dark and hairy, rarely are they scary.'" Or as you humans would say, "Don't judge a book by its cover!"

But that's easier said than done, especially when it comes to the story I'm about to tell you. . . .

Chapter 1

When Ponds Boil

What could be more relaxing than a sunny, lazy Sunday afternoon? There is nothing better than dangling upside down from a tree branch in Castle Park, Fogville's most beautiful park, and watching Fogville's citizens camped out on the lawn.

One spring day in particular, dozens of families had spread their blankets on the grass in the park. Clouds of butterflies crossed the bright blue sky. What a lovely sight!

The Silvers were enjoying the day in the park too. Mrs. Silver was picking up the leftovers from our picnic lunch. Mr. Silver was reading the paper. Michael, Becca, Tyler, and I wandered over to the pond to feed the fish.

"How can you throw away all those breadcrumbs?" Tyler complained. "I'm still hungry! What a waste!"

"Oh, knock it off, Tyler," Michael replied. "You already stuffed your face!"

Becca ignored her brothers. "Look at the size of this fish!" she said, pointing at the water. "It's huge!"

Tyler peered into the water to see what Becca was talking about. I thought about going to look too, but I was so tired. My eyelids were going up and down like window blinds. I heard Michael ask, "Anyone want to play Frisbee?" But a few seconds later, I was sound asleep.

Since my eyes were closed, I didn't see what was happening. The pond started to boil!

The kids were the first to notice. Then some grownups approached the small lake. A few minutes later, everybody was gathered around it, trying to figure out what was going on.

"Look at those bubbles, Mom! They're huge!" a little girl yelled enthusiastically.

"Cool!" one boy said. "Can I go swim, Dad?"

The Silver kids were staring at the lake in amazement. As they watched, the water continued to boil like a pot on the stove. Michael had to take off his glasses so he could see what was happening; they were completely fogged up. That could only mean one thing — trouble was on its way!

"Is it me, or is the lake changing colors?" Mr. Silver asked. "It's turning red . . . no, wait, orange . . . no, wait, yellow!"

"Cool!" Tyler said.

The only two people who weren't excited about the changing colors were Michael and Becca. They were too worried about the weird behavior of the fish. They both stood near the edge of the pond, looking pretty scared.

Suddenly, the fog that had formed over the water thickened. It went from being white and odorless to smelling like rotten eggs! It was disgusting.

As soon as the stench reached their noses, the crowd turned and stampeded out of the park. In less than five minutes, I was the only one left in that stinky, abandoned park. But I kept sleeping as if nothing had happened.

Chapter 2

Hit by a Frisbee

If it wasn't for Michael's Frisbee-throwing skills, I could have been poisoned by that awful smell. Luckily, as soon as my friends realized that I was still at the park, they bravely came back to find me.

Becca immediately spotted me, still hanging, among the leaves of the tree. "There he is!" she hollered, pointing at me.

"We're too late!" Tyler yelled. "He's already passed out!"

"I think he's just sleeping," Michael reassured him. "But we have to wake him up before the smell makes him sick."

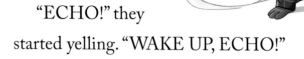

"ECHO!" they started yelling. "WAKE UP, ECHO!"

But I didn't even budge. I was dreaming of flying over the misty swamp where my old cousin Apnea used to live. He'd made his specialty for dinner: seaweed tortillas with fruit flies! I tried to tell him that the eggs he'd used must have been rotten, because the tortilla stank to high heaven.

He didn't take that very well. He threw the plate at me, hitting me square in the face!

I heard him say, "Nice shot, Michael!"

I woke up suddenly with a pounding headache. The fog had risen quite a lot, and it smelled like rotten eggs, just like my cousin's tortilla! Pee-whew!

I glanced up above me and noticed something stuck on a branch right above my head. Looking closer, I realized that it was the red plastic plate my cousin had thrown at me.

Wait a minute! I thought. *What am I doing hanging up in a tree?*

"Echo!" I heard someone call. That wasn't Apnea's voice. "Echo! It's me, Michael!"

"Michael who?" I wanted to ask, but I couldn't make a sound. The smell was too overpowering.

"Get down! Quick!" a girl added. "We have to get out of here!"

"And since you're up there, get my Frisbee too!" the boy added.

I tried to move my legs, but they felt like they were made of stone. I lost my grip and started falling to the ground. I closed my eyes, trying to prepare for the crash, when two soft hands caught me.

A girl with red bangs smiled at me. Over her shoulder, I recognized my cousin Apnea's swamp. At least I thought I did.

But why is it yellow? I wondered. *And why is it boiling like a pot of hot water?*

I didn't have time to ponder those questions for long. The girl holding me turned and ran out of the park. I kept my eyes on the pond as we ran. When we were about halfway across the park, I saw a large goldfish leap out of the water. His eyes were open wide with fear.

When he was at the peak of his jump, an enormous green hand emerged from the swamp.

It snatched the goldfish out of the air and pulled it back underwater.

And that's the last thing I remember.

Chapter 3

Fish Don't Drown

The next day, I woke up to find three worried faces staring down at me. I tried to put my surroundings into focus.

"Hi, kids!" I mumbled, recognizing my attic. "Did I miss anything?"

"Just my Frisbee," Tyler grumbled.

"Frisbee?" I asked. "What Frisbee?"

"Don't listen to him, Echo," Michael said. "We're just glad you're okay."

"What do you remember?" Becca asked.

"I remember the swamp," I began. "And the fog . . . and a terrible smell! And I also remember falling down, but someone caught me."

I was about to tell Becca the last thing I had seen before passing out. But then she handed me a big glass of kiwi shake, my favorite!

"Drink this," she said, smiling at me. "It will make you feel better."

"Hey, I'm feeling weak too," Tyler complained. "Where's my milkshake?"

"Oh, give me a break!" Michael said. "Hand me the newspaper. We have to tell Echo what happened."

That was exactly what I'd been about to ask before that delicious milkshake distracted me.

I put down my glass and picked up the front page of the *Fogville Echo*. There was a photo of the yellow pond and a full-page headline that read:

FEAR IN CASTLE PARK!
TOXIC SUBSTANCE POLLUTES POND!

That explained why I was feeling as limp as a wet noodle! *What was in that air I breathed?* I wondered. I was so weak that I had to ask Michael to read the article for me.

"Mr. Nibble, an engineer with the Municipal Sewage System, reassured citizens that everything will be okay," Michael read aloud. "'After a thorough investigation, we've discovered that the toxic substance came from a sewage pipe that runs close to the park,' Nibble said. 'The pipe cracked, and the pollutants spilled into the pond, killing all the fish. Fortunately, nobody was hurt. Technicians from a specialized company will now repair the pipe and drain the lake, and everything will go back to normal.'"

"Well, it sounds good if you believe that guy," I said. I looked over at Tyler, who was staring at my shake.

"Something doesn't add up," Michael said, folding the newspaper. "First of all, who put that stuff in the sewers? And was it really just a coincidence that the sewers spilled into the pond on Sunday, when the park was full of people?"

"There's something else bugging me," Becca said, opening the newspaper again. "Dead fish float. If all the fish in the pond were killed, why isn't there a single one in this picture? There were dozens of fish in the pond!"

"Maybe they drowned," Tyler suggested, his eyes still glued to my milkshake.

Both Michael and Becca looked at their brother like he was crazy.

In the meantime, I couldn't make up my mind. I wanted to tell them what I had seen, but I was afraid they would think I was crazy. I decided I had to speak up.

"Something is bothering me too," I suddenly said. "Before I passed out, I think I saw something coming out of the pond."

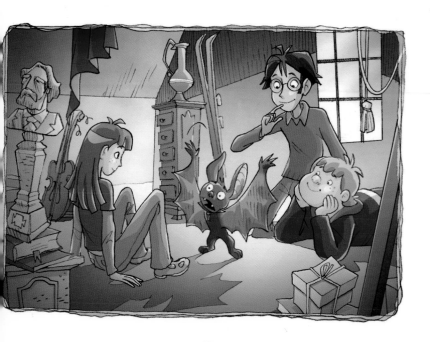

The Silver kids immediately looked at me. Only Tyler kept staring at the kiwi shake.

"What do you mean?" Becca asked.

"I might be wrong, but it looked like a big green hand!" I said. "It grabbed one of the fish and pulled it underwater."

"What?" Tyler stammered, finally shifting his gaze on me.

"A *green hand*?" Michael echoed, frowning. "What kind of green?"

"Like Tyler's face right now," I said.

Chapter 4

Nobody Likes
a Bully!

No one wanted to believe me. Tyler even asked me jokingly if I'd seen a red foot running around the park, too. I tried to tell them I was serious, but I had no proof.

"What time does the park close?" Michael asked, changing the topic.

"Six o'clock," Becca told him. "Why?"

"Perfect. We have the whole day to take a look around," he said. "Who's coming?"

Nobody was all that excited to go back to the park, but we all went anyway. (Tyler made it clear that he was only coming to retrieve his Frisbee.)

But when we got to the park, we realized looking around wouldn't be as easy as we'd thought. The area around the pond had been sealed off with police tape and signs that read, "Contaminated Area. No Trespassing."

A big tanker truck was parked off to the side of the pond. The writing on the side of the truck read, "B & C Cleaning — We Clean Up After You!"

The air smelled clean again, but the water was still as yellow as a lemon. At least it had stopped bubbling and gurgling. All around the pond, however, puddles had formed. Wherever the water had touched it, the grass had burned away.

"What a mess!" Becca exclaimed.

A big man wearing a black leather jacket and tinted sunglasses suddenly appeared in front of us. I barely had time to hide behind Becca.

"What are you kids doing here? Can't you read?" he snapped.

Becca glared at him. "Of course we can read," she snapped back. "The sign says 'No Trespassing.' We followed the instructions!"

The man looked surprised. Obviously he hadn't been expecting her to talk back to him. "You've got quite the smart mouth," he said. "What's your name?"

"Becca," she replied. "What's yours?"

"Bunker," he said. "Listen up. I don't need a bunch of nosy kids poking around. Why don't you kids go play somewhere else and let us work in peace? It's dangerous here."

"Are you here to clean the pond?" Michael asked.

"You're a regular Einstein, aren't you?" the man said sarcastically. "Now, scram. This is my last warning."

Just then, a stocky man with a face like a bulldog popped up behind him. "We're ready, boss!" he barked.

"Go ahead, Clinker," the man replied. Then he turned back to us. "You kids had better get outta here before I suck you up with the rotten water!"

Tyler was gone before the man had even finished his sentence. Becca wasn't so easy. She was furious.

"Who does that guy think he is?" she said. "He can't treat us like that just because we're kids!"

Michael grabbed Becca's arm and pulled her away too. "I hate to break it to you," her brother replied, "but he just did."

"That's not fair!" Becca replied, crossing her arms. "When I grow up I'm going to be a lawyer and stand up for kids who get treated like that!"

Michael, Tyler, and I looked at her in awe. Becca stared at the ground. She seemed a bit embarrassed by her outburst.

"Hey, come look at this!" she suddenly said. She crouched down to look at the ground.

We walked closer to see what she was looking at. A small goldfish (well, it was actually more purple than gold) was twitching helplessly in one of the puddles that had formed around the pond.

"Give me something to put the fish in!" Becca cried. "Fast!"

Reluctantly, Tyler handed his sister the plastic cup he'd been drinking out of. Becca quickly dumped out the soda and filled the cup with fresh water from a nearby fountain. She dropped the fish into it, and we took off for home.

We'd just reached the entrance to the park when my hypersensitive ears heard something. It sounded like a lullaby and seemed to come from a manhole in the middle of the street.

I flew over the manhole and hovered above it in midair, listening. There was no doubt about it. Someone was singing down there!

Just then, the roar of an engine drowned out everything else.

"Watch out, Echo!" Becca screamed.

I looked up to see a car headed right for me!

Chapter 5

Special Report!

Thank goodness for my cousin Limp Wing, who's a member of the Aerobatic Display Team! I owe him my life. Without the moves he taught me, I might not be alive today!

When I saw the car approaching, my sonar immediately told me how far away it was and how fast it was moving. I held my wings close to my body and took off at the last moment in a fantastic movement known as the "super-leapo vertical jump." Phew! I got out of the way just in the nick of time!

"Are you sure you weren't in the circus before we met you?" Tyler asked jokingly while I tried to catch my breath.

I frowned. "I heard someone humming down there," I told him. "In the sewer. I'm sure of it."

"Sure," Tyler said with a laugh. "Maybe it was a rat shaving!"

Michael and Becca gave me a worried look but didn't say anything. No one believed me!

By the time we made it back to the Silvers' house we'd come up with a lot of questions, but not one single answer.

"What a useless trip!" Tyler muttered. "I didn't find my Frisbee, and now my cup smells like fish!"

"Cut it out, Tyler!" Becca said. She was busy moving the purple fish to a small plastic fishbowl and giving it some food. "What was I supposed to do? I couldn't just leave this poor little thing there to die!"

"What are you going to do with it now?" Tyler asked. "Turn it into fish sticks?"

"I'm going to try to cure it," Becca said. "There has to be a way to get its color back."

You know Becca. When she sets her mind to something, she's as stubborn as an ox.

* * *

Over the next few days, Becca did everything she could to cure her new pet. She poured weird mixtures in the water and made special food. She even spent hours talking to the fish, despite Tyler teasing her about it.

As the days went by, we almost forgot about what had happened at the park that day. But one week later, there was another incident.

We were all sitting in the living room watching "Banana Man," Tyler's favorite cartoon about a tall, gangly superhero all dressed in yellow, when the show was interrupted by a special report.

"Hey! That's not fair!" Tyler complained.

"Oh, stop being such a baby, Tyler," Becca said. "Something serious might have happened."

Michael looked up from reading *Blood and Ketchup*, Edgar Allan Poultry's new horror novel. He turned up the TV.

"We interrupt regular programming to give you breaking news. Foul, reddish water is spouting out of Dolphin Fountain in downtown Fogville's Clocktower Square. The

40

area has been sealed off, and the police and fire departments are already on site. We now go live to our own Fred Oniontop. Can you hear me, Fred? What's the current situation there?"

On the TV screen, we could see a short bald man, looking very queasy and holding a handkerchief to his mouth. He was surrounded by a hazy red mist.

"As you can see," the reporter said, "the situation, *cough, cough*, is extremely critical. Clouds of smoke are now coming from the, *cough, cough*, substances that turned the fountain water red, making it very hard to breathe. *Cough, cough*."

"Do we know what caused this, Fred?" the news anchor asked.

"Dr. Nibble from the, *cough, cough*, Municipal Sewage System is here with us to take that

question," the reporter said. He turned to the man standing next to him and held out the microphone. "Sir, what can you tell us?"

"Jeez, that guy is everywhere!" Tyler commented.

"My technicians have just completed an extensive underground inspection," the engineer said in a funny, catlike voice. "It seems that the pollutants rotted one of the pipes near the fountain's plumbing system and spilled into the fountain's water, killing all the goldfish, unfortunately."

"Is it just me, or is that the same explanation he gave the last time?" I asked.

"And it's the second time that the fish disappeared without a trace," Becca said.

"Excuse, *cough, cough*, me, Dr. Nibble," the reporter, who was looking sicker by the minute, continued. "This is the second similar episode in just a few days, *cough, cough*. Doesn't it look suspicious to you?"

"It's more than suspicious," Michael muttered.

"Let's leave the investigation to the police," the engineer said. "My job is to reassure Fogville's citizens that there is absolutely no danger whatsoever to the city's drinking water. B & C

Cleaning will carry out the fountain drainage. Everything will be back to normal in no time."

"What a coincidence!" Becca said.

"We should go check things out at that fountain," Michael said. "But let's wait and go at night. I don't want to run into that man again."

"There's no point in all of us going," Tyler said. "All we need is someone who's good in the dark and can get an overhead view."

They all turned around to look at me.

I sighed. I knew they wouldn't stop bugging me until I agreed. There was only one problem.

"What if I see that green hand again?" I asked.

Chapter 6

Yucky Bugs

Nobody seemed to take my fears seriously.

Nobody except Tyler, that is. He took pity on me, probably because he'd been the one to suggest I go. He motioned for me to follow him upstairs. When we got to his bedroom, Tyler pulled a disgusting-looking insect from his desk drawer.

"I've been waiting to try this out!" he said excitedly. "Let me introduce you to my *bug*!"

"Nice to meet you," I replied. "Are you collecting beetles now?"

"Very funny!" Tyler said. "This isn't a real bug. It's a secret audio-monitoring device."

"A secret what?" I asked.

"It's a fake bug that has a microphone hidden inside," Tyler explained. "It'll pick up any sound within 100 feet. Get it?"

"Not really," I said. I usually didn't understand Tyler's inventions.

"It's going to help us figure out if that green hand and voice you thought you heard coming from the sewers are real or not," Tyler said. He held up the bug. "All you have to do is stick this thing under the lid of a manhole. If someone is really hiding down there, you and I will be the first to know."

"But how am I supposed to take the manhole lid off by myself?" I asked.

Tyler smirked. "Who said you have to take it off?"

* * *

I waited until it was dark to go on my night mission. Holding Tyler's fake bug in my hand, I flew to Clocktower Square. The town looked deserted as I flew overhead. Everyone was home, safe and sound, in their beds.

I circled Dolphin Fountain. The area around

the fountain was still sealed off. Judging by the clear look of the water, the guys from B & C had already finished their job. Obviously, there were no fish left in the fountain.

I'd just turned back when a loud *SPLASH!* sent a chill down my spine.

I flew higher to avoid being spotted and circled back to fly over the fountain again. I couldn't believe what I was seeing! Two large goldfish were splashing up and down in the fountain. Where had they come from?

Just then, I heard muffled thumping from near the fountain. It sounded like something was moving underground. The noise suddenly stopped. One of the manhole lids within the sealed-off area lifted up just a little and then closed again.

Scaredy-bat! What was I supposed to do?

Should I trust my gut and scram, or should I stay and carry out my mission?

Tyler's idea was simple. "Just aim for the little holes on the lid of the manhole," he'd told me. "The bug will drop right in. You won't even have to go near it yourself. It'll be easy!"

Easy, my wing! Fortunately, I remembered another trick my aerobatic cousin Limp Wing had taught me — the Jade Arrow. It was an extremely complicated maneuver used to hit a small target from a great distance.

I took a deep breath and hovered above the manhole that had moved. I started spinning in a tight circle. Then, holding the bug in my hand, I raised my arms over my head and dropped it!

Clink-clank-clang! The bug fell to the ground and bounced off the manhole. I'd missed the target! Now what was I going to do?

I didn't have time to come up with a plan. As I watched, the heavy metal manhole cover lifted up again. It creaked loudly in the silent square. From underneath the cover came a huge green hand!

The hand grabbed the bug, which had bounced a few feet away, and disappeared, closing the lid behind it.

Chapter 7

Cheeseburger

"Mission accomplished!" I exclaimed as I flew back into the attic.

Michael and Becca were asleep, but Tyler had waited up. He was already listening on the receiver.

"Can you hear anything?" I asked.

"No," Tyler said. "Are you sure you threw it into the manhole?"

"It's definitely in the manhole!" I replied. I

decided I didn't need to tell him exactly how it had gotten there.

"Then all we have to do is wait," he said. "You're on the graveyard shift. I'm going to sleep. But wake me up right away if you hear anything!"

For us bats, nighttime is like daytime for you humans. We're wide awake and as alert as swamp owls. But even I have to admit that listening to Fogville's underground sewers on a

pair of headphones isn't the best way to pass the time.

Drip! Drop! went the water in the sewer tunnels. The sounds reminded me of an old nursery rhyme that my mother had taught me when I was little. I started to hum it.

"Drop by drop, it's so funny

Li'l bat washes his own tummy . . ."

Oh, how I missed hearing my mother sing that song! I could almost hear my brothers' voices.

"Drop by drop, it's so funny,

Li'l bat washes his own tummy.

In the dark and pitch black cave

He is always happy and always brave!"

None of my brothers had such a deep voice,

though. I couldn't believe it! The voice was coming from the sewers!

I bolted into Tyler's bedroom to tell him what I'd heard. "Tyler! Wake up! I found it! Wake up!" I whispered.

I managed to wake up Michael and Becca, but Tyler wasn't so easy. He kept snoring like an eighteen-wheeler.

"What did you find, Echo?" Michael asked. He sat up in bed and put his glasses on.

"I . . . uh . . . I promised I'd tell Tyler first," I stammered. "But I can't wake him up!"

"You're trying to wake up Tyler?" Becca chimed in. "All you need is the magic word."

She went near him and whispered one simple word in his ear: "Cheeseburger."

Half a second later, Tyler sat up in his bed

and said, "I'll take a burger, well done, please, with BBQ sauce and a side of French fries."

By my grandpa's sonar! That kid never stopped surprising me!

"Echo!" he said as soon as he saw me. "What's going on?"

"I heard it, Tyler!" I told him. "It's down there!"

"What's down where?" Michael demanded. "Will one of you please tell us what's happening?"

"Let's go to the attic," Tyler said. "But be quiet. We don't want to wake up Mom and Dad."

Up in the attic, we took turns listening to the deep voice singing my nursery rhyme.

"Do you think the green hand belongs to the guy who's singing?" Becca asked.

"Who knows," Tyler replied. "We'd have to go down there to find out, and I, for one, am not that crazy."

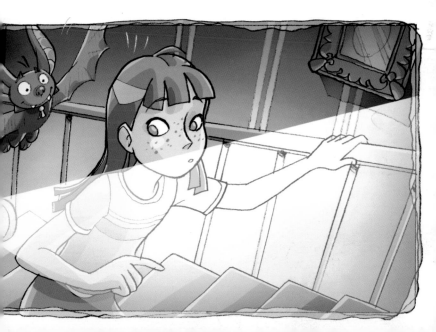

"Actually, we can all be a little bit crazy," Michael said. "Mom and Dad are going to a party at the Polka Club tomorrow night, and they'll be back late. We'll have all the time we need."

Tyler and I tried to argue, but Michael wouldn't take no for an answer. When he told Tyler to download the map of Fogville's sewers from the Internet, none of us had the courage to stop him.

Chapter 8

Flies, Rats, and Cockroaches

The next day, while Mr. and Mrs. Silver got ready for their party, Michael, Tyler, Becca, and I pretended that we had a pajama party, complete with movies and snacks, planned for the night. Tyler even made himself a huge bowl of popcorn to be extra convincing.

In reality, our pajamas were covering the dark clothes we all wore to blend into the night better.

When Mr. and Mrs. Silver finally left for their party, we made our move. We chose the most isolated manhole on Friday Street to descend into the sewers beneath Fogville's streets. According to Michael, Tyler's invention and the map of the sewers would lead us right to our goal.

Panting, Michael and Tyler lifted the heavy manhole cover, and we climbed down a ladder to the world below. When we reached the bottom,

we put our feet on a dimly lit narrow concrete sidewalk. A dark, slimy stream flowed next to it.

"Phew! This stinks!" Tyler complained. "This is disgusting!"

A family of disgusting black rats was staring at us suspiciously.

"How cute!" I joked. "They look like wingless bats."

"You'd better make sure they don't eat your wings!" Tyler warned me. He put on a pair of weird-looking headphones with an antenna. The headphones were connected to the bug.

"You look like a human fly!" Becca teased him, cracking everybody up.

"Laugh all you want, but remember that the human fly is your only hope down here," Tyler reminded her.

We started walking along the sidewalk, following the disgusting river upstream. We were all very careful not to touch the mold-covered walls and to step over the huge cockroaches that occasionally crossed our path.

"They're kind of cute, aren't they?" Becca giggled.

"Yuck!" Tyler said, sounding disgusted. He shook his head. "What did I do to deserve a sister like you?"

We walked along the underground sidewalk until we came across a smaller tunnel that branched off to the side. We were stuck. Michael and Tyler couldn't agree on the right way to go.

"Clocktower Square is to the left!" Michael said.

"I'm telling you, the signal is coming from the right!" Tyler argued.

"Will you two quit arguing already?" Becca snapped at them. "Look over there. What's that light?"

From the bottom of the smaller dark tunnel came a faint, glowing light and the noise of water falling.

"I told you the signal was coming from the right!" Tyler said victoriously.

"We have to go down there!" Michael insisted.

"But it's too dark!" Tyler complained. "What if we fall in the water? We could get eaten alive by crocodiles!"

"There are no crocodiles in the sewer!" Michael said, rolling his eyes.

"Why don't we let Echo go check it out?" Becca suggested. "He's the best when it comes to moving around in the dark."

What do you know? One compliment was all it took, and there I was, putting my wings on the line for someone else. When was I going to learn to say no?

But I knew I couldn't say no to Becca. After all, like my grandpa always used to say, "*Avoid the sun, keep up the speed, but never say no to a friend in need!"*

I flew close to the ceiling of the tunnel. When I was near the entrance, I hung from the stones jutting out from the ceiling and crawled slowly toward the light. This was another trick Limp Wing had taught me. He called it the "upside-down leopard walk."

As soon as I leaned into the tunnel to take a look, though, I was so shocked I almost fell off.

"Well?" Michael whispered from the end of the tunnel.

"The coast is clear!" I answered in a soft voice.

The Silver kids walked single file down the sidewalk to where I hung. But when they got to the bright opening, they gasped in amazement, just like I had.

Chapter 9

Sweet Just Like a Monster

Before us stood a huge cave filled with garbage. On the far wall, disgusting green water spewed out of a huge, rusty pipe and splashed into a large, rectangular tub.

The walls of the cave were covered with alcoves. Each alcove was filled with dozens and dozens of tubs holding fish of every shape and size. Every tub had a tag with a name written on it: Snory, Zorba, Reddy, Poppy.

"This must be the town's biggest aquarium!" Becca exclaimed.

"Who built this?" Michael asked.

"Whoever he is, he doesn't shower very often!" Tyler said, holding his nose. "It smells terrible!"

"Well, he obviously loves animals," Becca said, still admiring the fish.

Suddnely we were startled by Tyler shouting, "Look! My bug! How did it end up here?"

I could've answered that question, but I decided not to tell them about the green hand I'd seen snatch the bug.

Just then, a horrible growl shattered the silence of the cave! Scaredy-bat!

"Someone's coming!" I yelled. "And he doesn't sound happy!"

"I want Mom!" Tyler whimpered.

"Let's hide in there! Quick!" Michael said, pointing at a dark nook full of glass jars. Once we were safely hidden, I took a better look at the jars. They were filled with worms! The jars rattled as the earth shook. It sounded like a dinosaur was stomping in our direction! The footsteps came to a halt at the entrance to our hiding place.

What we saw was enough to make us almost wet our pants. Standing there was an enormous green monster covered in slime. Its arms and legs were as big as tree trunks, and it was

breathing heavily. He was so big that he blocked the entrance completely.

"Goodbye, everyone!" Tyler cried. "It was nice knowing you!"

The monster took a step forward, showing his ugly green face. Two angry eyes stared out at us above a flat, snotty nose and a huge mouth.

"Do you believe my story about the green hand now?" I whispered.

The monster lurched toward us, took one of the jars, and stopped to listen. Tyler's knees were shaking uncontrollably. As usual, Michael was the one who found a solution. He picked up a pebble and threw it across the cave. It pinged against one of the little tubs farthest away from us.

Hearing the noise, the monster turned around and growled in rage. When he didn't see anything, he calmed down. He started moving around the cave, feeding the fish. He tickled them with his big green fingers, and when they came up to eat, he giggled happily, singing, "Din-din! Din-din!"

"What a sweet guy!" Becca said with a sigh. Seeing someone taking care of animals always made her happy.

"Yeah, right," Tyler muttered. "So sweet he could eat us in one bite!" As he talked, Tyler forgot to be careful. He accidentally moved his leg, hitting a stack of jars that was behind him. They all crashed to the ground.

Now we were done for.

My Mommy!

Just like my grandma always used to say,
"*When bad comes to worse, the smallest chicken can
beat a horse!*"

In this case, Tyler was our chicken. As the
monster turned around and spotted us, Tyler
tried to joke his way out of trouble.

"Ha! Ha! Ha! You win!" he said, laughing.
"You found us! Good job, buddy!"

The giant stared at him, confused.

Tyler kept talking. "Of course you won! You're so smart. And handsome! I bet you can get any girl you want!"

The monster blushed and mumbled something.

Tyler turned toward us. "It worked!" he whispered. "He's falling for it!" He turned back to the monster and went on. "You should just take care of your looks a bit more. When's the last time you brushed your teeth? Your breath is terrible!"

The monster didn't like hearing that at all. He growled so loudly that the glass jars rattled on their shelves.

"Way to go, Tyler!" Michael said. "Now you made him really mad!"

"Let's try to sneak under his legs!" I suggested.

I was about to make a break for it, but Becca's voice made me freeze.

"NOBODY MOVE!" she hollered. She opened her backpack and pulled out a plastic bag. Inside the bag swam the weak gray fish she'd rescued.

"I saved it from the pond, just like you did with your fish," she told the monster. "It's still sick, though. Can you help me?"

The monster stared at her for a moment. Then he took the bag from her hands, gently put the fish in a tub, and poured a bluish liquid into the water. Finally, he set the tub underneath a rosy light and sat down on the floor to wait.

Becca sat down next to him. I looked over at Michael and Tyler, who shrugged before following Becca's lead and sitting on the ground.

The giant opened his mouth and showed off his horrible teeth. "What's your name?" he asked.

"I'm Becca!" Becca replied. "These are my brothers, Michael and Tyler."

The monster glared at Tyler. "He was rude!" the monster said.

"That's just the way he is. He's always joking," Becca explained. Tyler looked relieved. "What about you? Do you have a name?"

"No. I live alone," the monster said sadly. "With no one to talk to there's no need to have a name."

"Maybe we can help you find a nice name," Becca suggested. "What do you think, Echo?"

"A bat!" the monster said as soon as he saw me. "I used to have a friend that was a bat. She taught me the nursery rhyme I sing to all my fish."

As I listened, the monster began to quietly sing. "*Drop by drop, it's so funny, li'l bat washes his own tummy. . . .*"

I couldn't believe it! That was my song! "What was the bat's name?" I asked, with a lump in my throat.

"Gwendolyn!" the monster replied. "She was an all white bat!"

"That was my mom!" I exclaimed. What a

coincidence! But how could she have known this monster?

"Your mom?" the Silver kids all said at once, sounding confused.

"How is Gwendolyn?" the monster asked. "Where does she live? I want to know everything!"

"She hasn't lived in Fogville since she married my father, Demetrius," I told him. "We used to live in the attic of an old library. But then they moved to the roof of a church in Chesterton, a lovely seaside village. They're still living there, but I don't see them very often."

"You must go visit your mother," the monster ordered me. He pointed a big, dripping green finger at me. "And you must talk about me. Promise!"

"Um … oh … okay," I stammered. "I promise!"

"And now, if you wish, you can give me a name," the monster offered.

The Silver kids all gave me encouraging looks, but nothing I came up with seemed to work. I suggested Smelly and Drainy, but the monster grunted in dislike. Supergreen didn't work either.

When I finally suggested, "Grog," the monster stopped to think. He stared at me, and for the first time, he smiled.

"I like Grog! That's a good name. MY NAME IS GROOOG!" he bellowed, making the floor shake.

Just then, the monster seemed to remember what he'd been doing. He pulled Becca over to the tub where he'd put her sick fish.

"Look! Your fish is better now!" he said proudly.

We all turned around and stared in amazement. The fish was swimming happily, and its shiny scales had gone back to their original, healthy purple color.

Chapter 11

Dr. Grog

Grog told us that he had been living in the sewers for a long time and that he was friends with all the animals that ended up down there. "Once I even found a little turtle," he said. "Someone had thrown it away, and its leg was hurt. But I took care of it and healed it."

"You're amazing!" Becca told him. Clearly, anyone who took such good care of his pets was okay with her.

"Where do all these fish come from?" Michael asked.

"It's a very sad, tragic story," Grog told us, shaking his head. "The evil men tried to kill them."

"What evil men?" Michael asked.

"The ones that poisoned the pond in the park and the fountain," Grog said.

"You mean that wasn't an accident?" Tyler asked.

"Of course it wasn't an accident!" Grog exclaimed. "It's a huge scam, that's what it is! They pollute the water, and then the mayor is forced to shell out a ton of money to have it cleaned up. The men who pollute the water get paid to do the cleanup and get rich in the process!"

"Did you manage to save all the fish?" Becca

asked, looking very worried. I wasn't surprised that the animals were her top concern.

"Each and every one of them," Grog reassured her. "I used my shortcuts through the sewers and got them out of the water. They're here now. They're safe."

"Did you see the men's faces?" Becca asked.

Grog shook his head. "I didn't see them, but I heard them talking," he said. "One of the men said, 'We've been just kidding around so far. When the town sees what we do to their little river, they'll really be scared!'"

"They want to poison the Blue River?" Becca cried. "We have to stop them!"

"I'm happy to help," Grog said. He growled angrily. "I am very angry with those men!"

"Thanks, Grog!" Michael told him. "We're definitely going to need your help."

Just then, my hypersensitive ears picked up some suspicious noises in the distance. "Hush!" I whispered to my friends. "Do you hear that?"

They all listened closely. "I can't hear anything," Tyler said. "Echo, are you sure all this excitement didn't mess up your sonar?"

"The bat is right," Grog said. "I can hear it too. Follow me. But be quiet!"

Since I had the best hearing, I took charge of showing everyone where the noises were coming from. I perched on Grog's shoulder to lead the way.

But there was a little problem. Grog didn't seem to know how to take directions. When I said, "right," Grog went left. When I said, "left," Grog went right. We were moving farther away instead of getting closer!

I decided I'd better be more direct if we

wanted to get anywhere. I started saying, "this way," or "that way," and we finally started getting closer. We could even make out some of the voices.

Grog crouched and whispered his plan. "The tunnel splits into two here. We should split into two groups. I'll go right."

"Grog, that's actually left," I corrected him.

"That's right! Then I'll go this way, and the four of you will go that way," he told us. "We'll surround the intruders. They won't be able to escape out either way. Does it sound like a good plan?"

"Perfect!" Tyler said. "Can I come with you, though? I'd feel safer."

Grog nodded. "Okay, you're with me. Let's get moving."

Chapter 12

The Evil Men

Michael, Becca, and I watched as Grog and that scaredy-cat Tyler vanished into the darkness of the right tunnel. When they disappeared, we turned and took the right one.

The noises were getting closer. As we drew near, we could make out a whiny voice that said, "Move it! Do you want them to catch us red-handed?"

"What do we do?" I whispered.

"Let's wait till Grog is here," Becca suggested. "He'll take care of them!"

"Good idea," Michael said. "But we have to find out what they're doing. Someone should peek around the corner."

"I'll go," Becca volunteered.

Could I let my friend risk her life like that? Of course not! So, even though I was scared wingless, I took off.

When I reached the entrance to the cave where the intruders were gathered, I flew up to the ceiling and peered inside. There were three men standing around. Even though the light was dim, I could swear I had seen them somewhere before.

"Hey, boss," the bulldog-faced man said. "A bat just flew in here!"

"So what?" the one wearing the leather jacket

replied. "What's your problem? Don't tell me you're afraid of bats!"

"No, of course not," the first man said. "It's just that I've heard you'll go bald if they pee on your head!"

"What's the problem?" the boss man replied. "You're already bald! Ha! Ha! Ha!"

By my grandpa's sonar! I suddenly realized where I'd see the two men before. It was Bunker and Clinker, the two guys from B & C. From

the looks of things, they were definitely up to no good!

There was a stack of yellow barrels, each labeled with a skull and crossbones, piled along one wall of the cave. Bunker and Clinker seemed to be moving the barrels into a new pile near the stream that flowed next to them.

Suddenly a third man, who'd been hidden up until then, spoke up. "Move it, you two!" he snapped. "Do you want to get caught?"

"Take it easy, Mr. Engineer!" Bunker replied. "Just because you're the boss in this filthy place doesn't mean you can push us around. Why don't you sit down and have some *Nibbles*! Ha! Ha! Ha! *Nibbles* — get it?"

I gasped quietly. That's who the third man was! Dr. Nibble, the engineer and manager of the Municipal Sewage System! How could I have not recognized him before?

He must be in on it with the other two! I realized.

"Are you sure that this canal flows into the Blue River?" Bunker asked.

"I'm positive!" Nibble said. "Pour that filth in there and in an hour, the citizens of Fogville will have a nice carrot-colored river! This time they'll have to pay us a lot more if they want to have their river back to normal!"

Chapter 13

The Floating Ghost

I immediately went back to my friends to tell them what I'd heard.

"We can't wait around," Michael said. "If Grog doesn't show up, we'll have to go ahead on our own."

"Grog?" someone said from behind us. We turned around and we saw something white hovering in midair.

"What's that?" Michael said.

"It looks like a . . .
a . . . a ghost!" Becca
stuttered.

"It's not a ghost at
all!" I butted in. I could
hardly believe what I
was seeing. "That's my
mom!"

"Fur-ball!" she
exclaimed as soon as
she saw me.

"Mom!" I yelled, throwing myself into her
wings. "What are you doing here?"

"Well, since you never come see us, I decided
I'd better come to see you," she replied, hugging
me back.

"How on earth did you know I was down
here?" I asked.

She smiled. "Actually, I didn't," she said. "I went to your old crypt at the cemetery first, but you weren't there. When I couldn't find you, I came down here to get some information from an old friend. Unfortunately, I haven't found him either."

"You must be talking about Grog, our big green friend. Don't worry. He's on his way," I told her.

"Really?" she said. "Oh, how lucky! I'm so happy!"

Just then, my mom noticed the Silver kids, still staring at her in shock. "Goodness, Fur-ball, where are your manners?" she exclaimed. "Why don't you introduce me to your friends while we wait for him."

I turned and introduced Becca and Michael to my mother. It was a little odd, introducing her to part of my new family! We'd just finished introductions when the noises from the tunnel brought us back to reality. I quickly filled my mother in on what was happening.

"There's only one thing we can do," she said. "We have to push over the barrels and hit those thugs with them!"

"How are we going to do that?" Michael asked. "They're too heavy!"

"Fur-ball," my mother said, "do you still remember the Achilles' Heel maneuver?"

"Sure, I do. But you're not thinking what I think you're thinking, are you?" I asked.

"Why not?" my mom asked. "The two of us should be able to make it. Let's give it a shot!"

Holding hands, my mother and I flew up to the ceiling of the cave. We set our sights on the first barrel on the left, which already seemed a

little unstable. We counted to three and then
flew straight toward our target. Michael and
Becca stared in amazement.

There was a loud *BANG!*

"What was that?" Dr. Nibble asked. A
second later, he was hit by a landslide of yellow
barrels. The barrels knocked him, and both of
his partners, into the water.

"We did it!" I yelled. "Becca, Michael, look,
we did . . ." My voice trailed off as I looked

around. There was no sign of my friends. The barrels had hit them too!

"Stay here!" my mother said. "I'll get them!" Before I could stop her, she'd taken off after them.

Chapter 14

Barrel Race

As my mother flew away, Grog and Tyler emerged out of the other tunnel. They looked exhausted.

"What took you two so long?" I asked. "I need your help!"

"It's his fault," Grog said, pointing at Tyler and scowling. "He kept making me confuse right and left!"

"That's not true!" Tyler argued. "You're the one who kept going the wrong way!"

"Stop it!" I hollered, interrupting their argument. "Michael and Becca fell into the water with the criminals. We have to go save them!"

Luckily, one of the barrels was still there, floating in the muddy water.

Grog climbed on top of the barrel, taking Tyler with him. He gave himself a push and set off after Michael and Becca.

If we hadn't been risking our lives, that barrel race might have been fun. It was like being on a rollercoaster! Grog kept zigzagging from one side of the canal to the other, shouting happily, "I like this game! I haven't had so much fun in a looong time!"

"Can't you slow down just a little?" Tyler

begged him. "I don't think it's safe to be going this fast!"

But Grog didn't even hear him. He just kept zigzagging happily.

We soon found Becca and Michael, who had managed to climb on top of the same barrel.

"Are you okay?" I yelled as we got closer.

"We're fine!" Becca replied. "But if your mom hadn't led us to the barrels, we would have been in real trouble!"

Wow! I thought. *We sure are lucky my mom was here!*

"Look!" Michael said, pointing downstream. "We almost have them!"

Not far from us, the three criminals were sitting on a barrel, screaming.

"I'll get you noooow!" Grog bellowed, making

them turn around. When the three men saw the enormous green monster coming toward them, they panicked. All three started paddling frantically, trying to escape.

But Grog was too fast for them. He was getting closer and closer. He reached out a huge hand to grab them. It seemed almost too easy!

As a matter of fact, it was. Things didn't go as planned!

A few feet ahead, the canal split into two. One led to a big waterfall, directly into Fogville's river. The other led into an extremely dark, narrow tunnel.

"Watch out!" I yelled, trying to speak loudly enough to be heard over the noise of the water. I could hear Tyler up ahead, begging Grog to slow down.

But instead of listening, Grog went faster. He reached the three criminals, who were doing all they could to stop. Grog went past them and came to a stop at the edge of the waterfall. Using one hand to stay hooked to the wall, Grog reached out his other hand to grab the criminals.

"They're going to hit us!" I screamed.

But Grog was one step ahead of me. Right as the criminals were about to hit us, Grog raised his leg and kicked their barrel as hard as he could. The force of the kick sent them flying out the other end of the tunnel. We heard them scream, and then there was silence.

Grog did the same thing to Michael and Becca, who were coming toward us at full speed. Wow! He was a real force of nature!

Finally, he tried to repeat the same process with us. But sometimes even forces of nature slip. Grog fell backward, and our barrel shot forward into the dark tunnel.

My mom desperately tried to grab on to it with her pale hands, but she was pulled away!

"MOM!" I yelped, trying to fly after her. But Tyler was holding me back.

"Don't be crazy, Echo! I'm sure she'll be fine," he tried to reassure me.

I felt like crying, but I didn't even have time. A second later, our barrel fell into the darkness.

Tyler and I hugged each other, screaming in terror.

Chapter 15

A Surprise Shower

We were spun around like clothes in a washing machine for what felt like days. We couldn't tell up from down, or right from left (something that had already caused us a lot of trouble)!

Finally the water slowed down, and we heard the noise of a waterfall. We flew out of the tunnel and landed in a large rectangular pool.

I would have drowned if someone hadn't grabbed me and lifted me out of the water.

"Look, boss!" a man said. "It's that bat again!"

I was so exhausted after my ordeal that I almost didn't recognize Clinker's bulldog face. He was holding me up with one arm and using his other arm to hold Michael still. Across the cave, Bunker had grabbed Becca and Tyler to make sure they couldn't escape.

Dr. Nibble, who was soaked to the skin in filthy water, was looking around, trying to figure out where exactly he was.

A glance at the dozens of lit fish tanks lining the walls told me that we were back in Grog's cave. But the monster was nowhere to be

seen. And neither was my mother! Where could they be?

"Can somebody tell me where we are?" Dr. Nibble snapped. "Who are these brats who ruined our plans?"

"They're a bunch of nosy kids who've been snooping in our business from the beginning," Bunker explained. "I think it's time to get rid of them once and for all."

"How?" Dr. Nibble asked as he tried to wring dirty water out of his shirt.

"How would you like to go for a swim in this lovely pool, kids?" Bunker asked with an evil chuckle.

"Maybe your bat friend can come with you," Clinker added. "Be careful, though. Nasty accidents can happen in pools. . . ."

"You're not going to get away with this!" Becca

shouted, struggling to break free. "Someone will find out what you did!"

"Maybe," Bunker said. "Too bad you won't be here to find out! Grab that rope, Clinker."

We had to do something — and fast! Without giving it a second thought, Becca sank her teeth into Bunker's hand and took off running, pulling Tyler behind her. Michael put his seven years of martial arts training to good use. He hit Clinker right in the stomach with a triple elbow smash.

The thug let me go, but not for long. They quickly took off after us. Bunker seemed to be the most furious. He picked up a heavy metal bar and ran after Tyler.

"Help me, Echo!" Tyler cried. "Heeelp! Do something! Please!"

What could I do?

Just then, I had a great idea. I was going to show those crooks that they were wrong about bats. Right then and there I came up with a brand-new aerobatic stunt: "The Surprise Shower."

As soon as Clinker felt the first warm drops land on his head, he looked up and started

screaming. "Yuck!" he yelled. "He peed on my head! That bat peed on my head!"

He held up his arms, trying to hit me, while his partner kept taunting him. "You'll go bald!" Bunker said. "You'll go bald!"

Just then, Dr. Nibble spoke up. "What is that?" he cried.

A huge green hand emerged from the water and set a white bat, soaked but alive, on one side of the pool.

"Mom!" I cried, flying toward her.

A second green hand grabbed on to the edge of the pool. Grog's head emerged from the water, followed by the rest of his body. He was back, and he didn't look happy!

Clinker and Nibble were terrified at the sight of that enormous monster. Bunker tried to swing the metal bar he was still holding to defend himself. That was a mistake. He accidentally hit some of the fish tanks instead.

Grog let out a terrifying *ROAR!* The three criminals quickly lost the little hair they had left.

The rest happened so quickly that they didn't even have time to fight back. Grog quickly immobilized the criminals.

When he was through with them, Grog took care of his fish. And with our help, he managed to save them all.

Chapter 16

A Green Face

No matter how hard they tried, the police could not explain who'd tied a metal bar, complete with a bow in front, around the three criminals.

Nor could they figure out how they'd ended up in front of the police station, sitting on a pile of yellow barrels, with a note that read:

Here are the men responsible for poisoning the pond at Castle Park and Dolphin Fountain. They were planning to spill the liquid contained in these barrels into Fogville's river. Fortunately, we stopped them in time!

The police didn't even have to interrogate the men. They immediately confessed and asked to be sent to Black Gate, the city jail. They all wanted to be locked up on the top floor, as far away from the sewers as possible. When the judge asked them why, they wouldn't answer.

That night, after the three criminals had been dealt with, we finally managed to finish our introductions. The Silver kids were excited to finally meet my mother. Tyler was even more excited to find out that she's a great cook — her fruit fly pie is terrific!

Grog was so happy to have found her again that he was close to tears. He kept repeating, "Gwendolyn is back! Gwendolyn is back!"

"Do you still remember the lullaby I used to

sing you before you went to sleep, Grog?" my mother asked him.

"Of course!" Grog replied. He started to sing it in his deep voice, and my mother joined in.

"Drop by drop, it's so funny,

Li'l bat washes his own tummy . . ."

Grog lay down, closed his eyes, and fell asleep like a baby.

The Silver kids and I never talked to anyone about our new friend. For one thing, we didn't want to sound crazy. But also because that was the best way to make sure he could keep living in peace.

The hardest part of the whole adventure was saying goodbye to my mother again.

"Come see me sometime!" she said before she left. "And bring your friends, too!"

"I will," I said, thinking of the vow I'd made to Grog. I knew he'd make sure I kept my promise.

* * *

After our adventure, things returned to normal. Becca wanted a fish tank for her birthday, but she didn't want any fish. She told her parents that she didn't need them. She was going to get some fish from a friend of hers who knew a lot about fish.

One night, she snuck out and slipped into the familiar manhole. The next day, ten little goldfish were swimming in her tank.

Mrs. Silver complained about the live worms that Becca was feeding her fish. But Becca told her that nothing was better for goldfish to eat. Her friend had told her that!

The town of Fogville held big celebrations for the reopening of Dolphin Fountain and the pond at Castle Park. The Silver family and I went to both ceremonies. At both events, the mayor gave a speech thanking the anonymous citizen responsible for putting the beautiful goldfish back in the water.

Michael, Tyler, Becca, and I couldn't hold back our laughter, even when Mr. and Mrs. Silver glared at us.

The following Sunday, we went back to the park for another wonderful picnic. This time, Mr. and Mrs. Silver decided to play Frisbee. They were even better than us!

While their parents played, the Silver kids relaxed. Tyler lay on his back, napping and snoring with his mouth open. Michael was reading the last chapter of *Blood and Ketchup*, Edgar Allan Poultry's new novel. Becca was busy talking to the fish in front of a crowd of amazed children.

I let out a big yawn and flew back to the leafy branches of my tree. I immediately fell asleep.

I had a wonderful dream about my mom teaching Grog the nursery rhyme. But she always stopped before the third verse! How frustrating! How did the third verse go?

Suddenly I woke up with a start. It was dark, and I was alone in the deserted park. A weird mumbling was coming from the direction of the pond.

I peeked through the leaves. This time I wasn't scared when I saw an enormous green monster paddling around in the water with his beloved fish. He was singing our lullaby!

I fluttered over to where Grog was. He was very happy to see me. I started singing with him.

"Drop by drop, it's so funny,

Li'l bat washes his own tummy . . ."

Without even thinking, the third verse just came to me.

"If the face he sees is green

He will know it isn't mean!"

Grog smiled at me. Year later, I finally got it. The lullaby was about him! My mother had been telling me that you couldn't tell if someone was good or bad just based on appearance.

Not bad, huh? I like it. And you know what? I think I'll use it for my next book. What do you think?

A "monstrous" goodbye,

Echo

ABOUT THE AUTHOR

Roberto Pavanello is an accomplished children's author and teacher. He currently teaches Italian at a local middle school and is an expert in children's theatre. Pavanello has written many children's books, including *Dracula and the School of Vampires*, *Look I'm Calling the Shadow Man!*, and the Bat Pat series, which has been published in Spain, Belgium, Holland, Turkey, Brazil, Argentina, China, and now the United States as Echo and the Bat Pack. He is also the author of the Oscar & Co. series, as well as the Flambus Green books. Pavanello currently lives in Italy with his wife and three children.

SEARCHING IN THE SEWERS

The Bat Pack and I saw a lot of disgusting things on our adventure through Fogville's sewers. Some of them are listed below. Can you find them in the wordsearch?

- MANHOLE
- MONSTER
- RATS
- SPIDERS
- STINK
- TUBES
- TUNNEL
- WATER
- WORMS

R	T	S	X	O	U	I	K	R	Z	M	U	Z
L	E	O	T	I	X	S	B	P	U	Y	U	U
E	G	T	W	I	P	M	A	N	H	O	L	E
N	S	M	S	I	N	Y	M	I	Q	B	U	W
N	R	E	D	N	R	K	G	O	H	J	A	N
U	P	E	B	A	O	T	M	J	Z	T	F	P
T	R	P	T	U	V	M	L	T	E	A	C	A
S	Z	S	G	T	T	H	R	R	D	S	Y	O
S	M	R	O	W	A	O	J	R	V	Y	Y	W
S	Z	T	B	W	X	I	L	H	A	B	G	H
G	J	Y	G	C	O	V	Q	F	S	A	K	D
L	K	M	M	A	E	V	P	H	Q	E	R	A
C	A	N	O	I	T	G	S	Y	E	W	R	B

THE THING FROM THE SEWERS

Things you'll need:

- glue
- newspaper
- green paint
- a paintbrush
- a plastic bag
- a black permanent marker

1. Cut the newspaper paper into thin strips, and place them in a bowl with two cups of water and two cups of glue. Stir until you have a smooth mixture.

2. Form the mixture into a ball, lay the plastic bag on the floor, and set the ball on it. Shape it into a monster and let it dry.

3. Paint your monster green, and use a black permanent marker to draw its mouth and eyes. Your Thing from the Sewers is ready!

AN ESCAPE ROUTE

Help! My sonar has failed me, and I'm lost! Can you help me follow a pipe of the sewers without getting caught in the evil clutches of Bunker and Clinker?

Check out more Mysteries and Adventures with Echo and the Bat Pack